NORA

The Fifty-Cent Dog

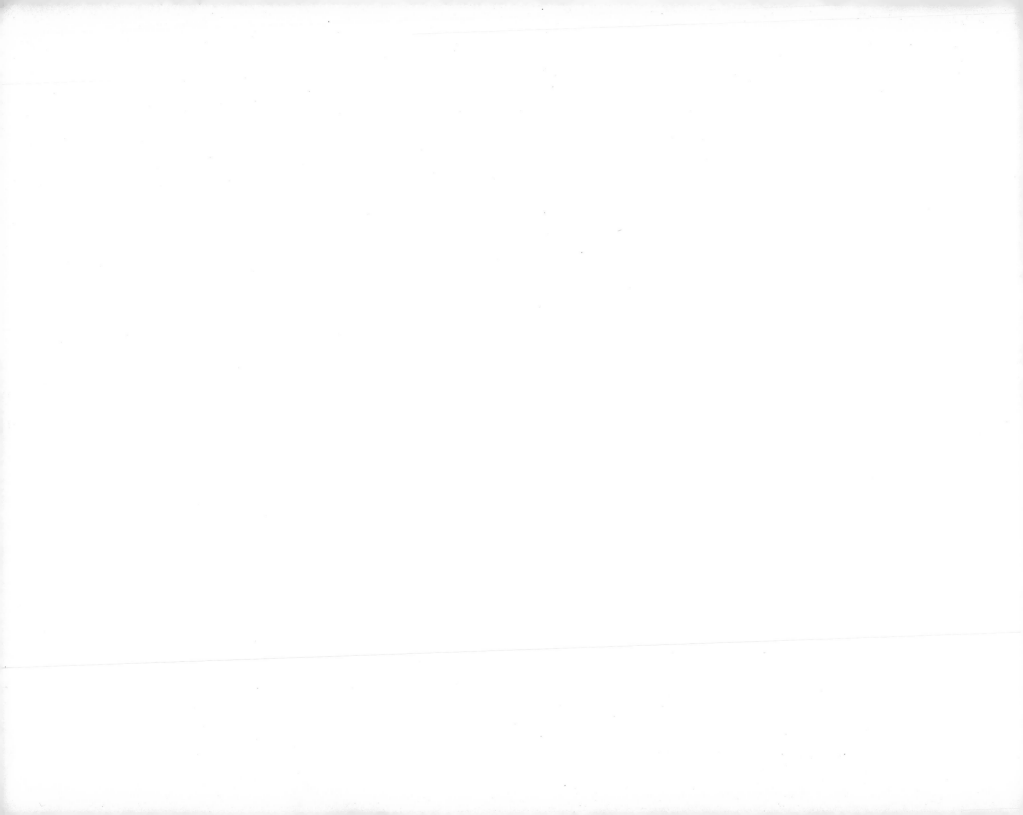

NORA
The Fifty-Cent Dog

written and illustrated

by

Lolly Stoddard

MYSTIC SEAPORT®
THE MUSEUM OF AMERICA AND THE SEA™

In memory of the dogs our family has loved: Piggy, Cindy-Lou Britches, Mosa McTavish, Amber, Charlie, Fifi, Hershey, Pete, Nicky, and Mickey.

Mystic Seaport
75 Greenmanville Ave., P.O. Box 6000
Mystic, CT 06355-0990

Manufactured in the United States of America

First edition

This is a work of fiction, inspired by an actual event. Except for Nora, names have been changed and details of the story have been interpreted by the author/illustrator.

The illustrations were done in watercolor with pen-and-ink details. The typeface is Baskerville.

ISBN 0-939510-87-1 (paper)
ISBN 0-939510-88-X (cloth)

It was a cold, stormy November night, and the waves were crashing at the ocean's edge. Jimmy walked the beach south of Oregon Inlet on North Carolina's Outer Banks. It seemed like the most secluded beach in the world.

World War II was being fought across the ocean. All along the shores of America, Coast Guardsmen like Jimmy patrolled the exposed beaches with their trained dogs, watching for any signs of enemy attackers trying to come ashore. On North Carolina's Outer Banks the threat was real. In past months,

Coast Guardsmen could see the smoke of ships set afire by enemy submarines. If submarines tried to land saboteurs, the patrol dogs were ready, with keen eyes and noses, to find the enemy and attack.

With the cold making Jimmy's mind wander, he remembered the day, seven months earlier, when the dog by his side became his partner on patrol. It was warmer then, and Jimmy had been strolling in town on liberty from the Coast Guard station when he saw the stray German shepherd, looking tired and hungry.

When she looked at him and wagged her tail, she won Jimmy's heart. Hanging off the dog's shabby collar was a disc with her name engraved on it. When Jimmy called out, "Nora," the dog jumped up and landed a juicy kiss on Jimmy's face! Jimmy decided to bring Nora back to the station, hoping that the crew would want to adopt her as a mascot.

Jimmy went to the dog pound to see if he could claim Nora. He reached into his pocket and pulled out his last two quarters to offer as payment.

"Because there is no fee for a dog in these parts, and no one has ever paid for a stray before, I can say that Nora is yours!" the pound-keeper exclaimed as he took the fifty cents.

"Fifty cents. . . fifty cents! I cannot believe I just bought a dog for fifty cents," Jimmy happily remarked to himself during the trip back to the remote station on the outer beach. Little did Jimmy know how special this dog would be.

Nora became more than a mascot. She followed Jimmy wherever he went. Although she had not gone to school for beach patrol dogs, she quickly learned what Jimmy taught her about being brave and watchful on the beach. Soon she was as skilled as the patrol dogs who had gone through the Coast Guard's training school.

This night on the beach, Jimmy and Nora had already walked more than a mile through the soft sand, up above the breaking surf. Coming back up the beach in the face of the northeast wind, Jimmy shivered as the cold worked its way through his body. His fingers and toes were numb, making him wonder if he would ever feel them again. Suddenly feeling light-headed and disoriented, Jimmy stumbled and fell. His mind went as black as the night.

The tide was rising toward Jimmy as he lay unconscious.
He was in danger of dying, and Nora whimpered and
nosed at him. Her master was in trouble—she would have
to get help fast! Nora grabbed Jimmy's arm and dragged
him away from the oncoming surf. Then she snatched
Jimmy's hat and raced back to the station to find someone
to help.

"Has Jimmy come back?" the lieutenant asked from his office in the Coast Guard station. "He called in from the post on the beach almost an hour ago. He should be back here by now. We need to know what he has seen."

"No, sir, he has not come in yet," replied one of the Coast Guardsmen.

No one in the station knew that Jimmy had collapsed. No one knew the danger that was upon him. . . no one except Nora, the fifty-cent dog.

"Get a party together to search the beach," the lieutenant ordered.

Just as the men were putting on their coats they heard some wild barking! Nora was jumping at the door and yelping. The men opened the door to find Jimmy's hat at Nora's feet. The dog was trying desperately to report that Jimmy was in danger and needed their help.

"Lieutenant, Nora knows where Jimmy is! Go, girl! We'll follow you."

The men raced after Nora as she bounded through the dunes to the ocean beach. Still holding Jimmy's hat, Nora dashed on ahead, followed by the beams of flashlights. Nora smelled another Coast Guardsman patrolling the beach and ran on to get him. The rescue party became winded as they ran through the sand, but at last they could see a dark shape on the beach with Nora dancing around it and barking as the other patrolman bent over to check Jimmy.

When the men reached Jimmy, they found Nora tugging at him and licking his face. Jimmy moved his arm and slowly opened his eyes. Nora crouched down against him, as if she knew he needed warmth until the others arrived to carry him back to the station.

As Jimmy was carried into the station on a stretcher, the other Coast Guardsmen cheered Nora and playfully put Jimmy's cap on her head. Nora barked with excitement. Then, another Coast Guardsman headed out with his dog so the beach patrol would continue without interruption.

The storm passed, and after recovering in the hospital with Nora by his side, Jimmy returned to patrolling the beach with Nora. Yet, this patrol dog now had become a celebrity. The story of her brave rescue efforts was told and retold throughout the Coast Guard. It became national news. Homeless Nora, the fifty-cent dog, had become known as Nora the brave defender of her country and its servicemen!

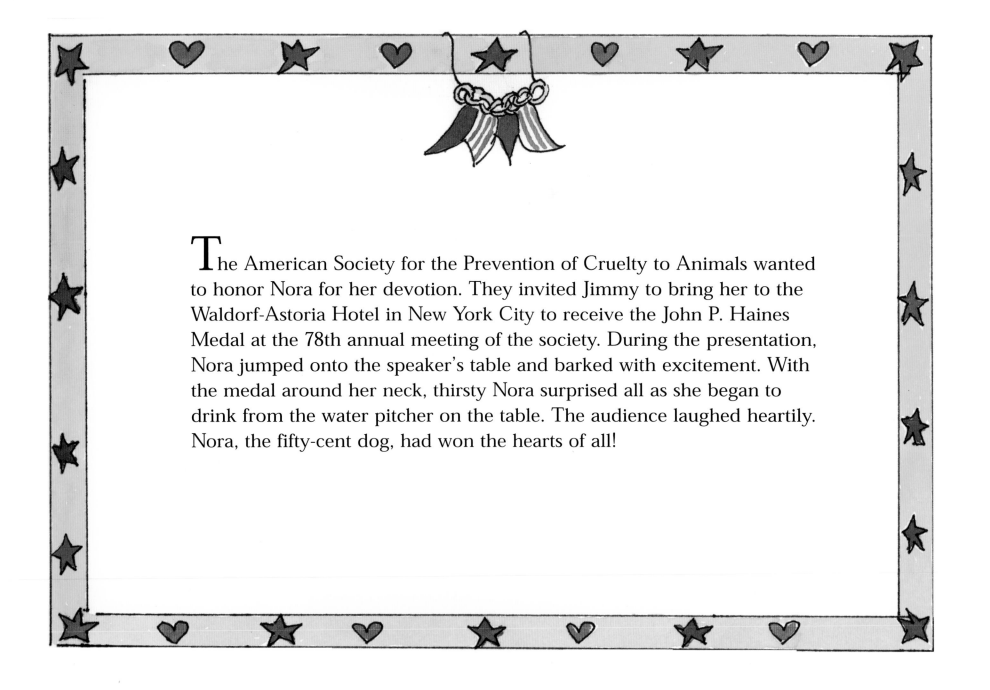

The American Society for the Prevention of Cruelty to Animals wanted to honor Nora for her devotion. They invited Jimmy to bring her to the Waldorf-Astoria Hotel in New York City to receive the John P. Haines Medal at the 78th annual meeting of the society. During the presentation, Nora jumped onto the speaker's table and barked with excitement. With the medal around her neck, thirsty Nora surprised all as she began to drink from the water pitcher on the table. The audience laughed heartily. Nora, the fifty-cent dog, had won the hearts of all!

Afterword

After enemy saboteurs were discovered on a Long Island beach in 1942, the U.S. Coast Guard patrolled the nation's exposed beaches with dogs from August 1942 to May 1944. During those 21 months, more than 2,600 Coast Guardsmen were trained to handle dogs, and more than 3,600 dogs served in the Coast Guard.

The inspiring facts of this story, which occurred at the Oregon Inlet, North Carolina, Coast Guard station in November 1943, are represented here to the degree that they are known. Nora was the actual name of the dog, but the seaman's name has been changed in the story to protect his privacy.

Further Reading

Eleanor C. Bishop, *Prints in the Sand: The U.S. Coast Guard Beach Patrol During World War II* (Missoula, Montana: Pictorial Histories Publishing Company, 1989).

"Coast Guard Beach Patrol During World War II," http://www.uscg.mil/hq/g-cp/history/Beach_Patrol_Photo_Index.html

Frederick Simpich, "Your Dog Joins Up," *National Geographic* 83:1 (January 1943): 93-113.

For my husband, Duncan.
Thank you for the enthusiastic support and love you always give me.
You are the wind beneath my wings.

For my children, Christy and her husband Craig,
Andrew, and John.
Thank you for your cheering encouragement.
It allows my wings to grow.

For my parents.
Thank you for your unconditional love.

Acknowledgments

I want to thank the following people at Mystic Seaport for their enthusiastic guidance as I developed
Nora, The Fifty-Cent Dog: Andrew German, Dede Wirth, and Linda Cusano. I also want to thank Mary Anne Stets,
Louisa Watrous, and Christopher Freeman for their support. Special thanks go to Bill Peterson for his long friendship
and for introducing Mystic Seaport to my first book, *Town Small*.

Lolly Stoddard is a well-known artist in the shoreline area of Connecticut, where she resides with her husband, whom she has known since childhood. She taught school for five years before concluding her teaching career to be at home with her children, all three of whom are now grown. Her artistic endeavors grew along with her children, and her memories of their creative imaginations have helped enliven her children's books. Her first book, *Town Small,* was published by Mystic Seaport in 2002 and is now in its second printing.

If you liked *Nora, The Fifty-Cent Dog* you might enjoy these other books from Mystic Seaport.

Town Small, written and illustrated by Lolly Stoddard, is a charming look at a coastal community and its busy seasons. Read along as this little seaside town fills with summer visitors and boats, and the drawbridge goes up and down at the heart of town.

32 pages, 17 illustrations, ISBN 0-939510-77-4 (paper) $9.95

What is a Sea Dog?, written by John Jensen and illustrated by Richard J. King, is inspired by the exhibit *Sea Dogs! Great Tails of the Sea*, at Mystic Seaport. Join little Skipper, a curious puppy in an orange life preserver, as she meets a galaxy of sea dogs from past and present. *What is a Sea Dog?* combines poetry, history, and fun in a celebration of the many dogs who love the water.

24 pages, 27 illustrations, ISBN 0-939510-81-2 (paper) $4.95

Mystic Seaport—The Museum of America and the Sea—is the nation's leading maritime museum, presenting the American experience from a maritime perspective. Located along the banks of the historic Mystic River in Mystic, Connecticut, the Museum houses extensive collections representing the material culture of maritime America, and offers educational programs from preschool to postgraduate.

For more information, call us at 888-9SEAPORT, or visit us on the Web at *www.mysticseaport.org*